ELSIE

To the fairies and other friends
—Ana Sender

Ana Sender was born in Terrassa (Barcelona), Spain, in 1978. She studied fine arts and illustration at the Massana Art School in Barcelona and completed her studies at the Francesca Bonemaisson School. She draws, writes, and imagines all sorts of stories. Her works have appeared in many books and newspapers. Ana lives near the forest. Many of her illustrations are inspired by her dreams. She likes werewolves, wild things, and green swampy places.

First published in the United States, Great Britain, Canada, Australia,
and New Zealand in 2019 by NorthSouth Books, Inc., an imprint of NordSüd Verlag AG,
CH-8050 Zürich, Switzerland.

Distributed in the United States by NorthSouth Books, Inc., New York 10016.
Library of Congress Cataloging-in-Publication Data is available.
ISBN: 978-0-7358-4338-7 (trade edition)
1 3 5 7 9 • 10 8 6 4 2
Printed in Latvia
www.northsouth.com

FSC
www.fsc.org
MIX
Paper from
responsible sources
FSC® C002795

THE COTTINGLEY FAIRIES

ANA SENDER

North
South

When we were little, my cousin Elsie and I spent summer afternoons in the forest. Not just the afternoons. And not just summer. Mornings too, and some nights, and autumn—and most of the time that we weren't at school . . .

But my favorite time was summer evenings. . . . We swam
in the stream, climbed the trees. We napped in the shade
and played with the creatures of the forest.

Adults lived in a very different world. . . .
It was hard and sharp, and they weren't able to see ours.

"If only they could see what we see . . ."
"Through the curtain."
"Through a gap."
"Or through a window."
"Taking photos is like opening windows," Elsie said.
And that's what we did.

I wish fairies would make things easier.

Although then they wouldn't be fairies.

Luckily, we had imagination,
pencils, paper, and scissors.

We did it: we photographed the fairies.

Without expecting it, lots of people paid attention
to us. Among them a famous writer called Arthur.

He liked mysteries and believed in fairies.
He wrote pages and pages defending the
authenticity of our photos.

A STUDY IN
SCARLET

THE ADVENTURES OF
SHERLOCK HOLMES

THE HOUND OF THE
BASKERVILLES

THE VALLEY
OF FEAR

Soon people from different places began to arrive.

They looked and looked, but saw nothing.

More and more people came,
and we found it difficult to
spend time with the fairies. . . .
Climbing.
Playing.
Breathing.

We told the people part of the truth:
the scissors and paper, that is.

They thought this was the whole truth.

Little by little the people left . . .
   returning to their everyday lives.

But the forest
seemed different.

We looked in every corner.

When the fairies finally appeared, we approached cautiously.

Little by little we managed to gain back their trust.

Many years have now passed. Almost everything has changed, and sometimes I find it hard to distinguish memories from dreams.

I just know that both of them
really happened.

This story is based on the events that took place
in England around the end of World War I. A series of photographs
caught the attention of the society of the time. The photos had been
taken by Elsie Wright and Frances Griffiths in the summer of 1917,
by the stream near their home in Cottingley (Yorkshire).

The pictures showed the two girls playing with several fairies.

It was Elsie's mother, Polly Wright, who first revealed the pictures in 1919
at a meeting of the Theosophical Society of Bradford. At that time, the interests
of these types of organizations in supernatural subjects were quite common.

Perhaps the matter would have remained only an anecdote had it not been
brought to the attention of the well-known writer Arthur Conan Doyle. Doyle, who,
after the death of one of his children, became obsessed with spiritualism and occultism,
defended the authenticity of the photos and was responsible for disseminating them
across different media. He wrote an article for The Strand Magazine *and talked*
about this subject at various conferences, in addition to sending copies of
the photos to several experts in order to prove their authenticity.

The impact was enormous, but opinions were divided. Many considered
that the photos had been doctored; others firmly believed that they were real. . . .
In 1981, well into their twilight years, Elsie and Frances confessed in an interview
that everything had been a montage, just a game. They had used pinned
paper clippings to take the images.

However, until her death in 1986, Frances Griffiths maintained that one
of the photos was indeed real and that fairies, of course, really do exist.